No Dogs Allowed

A TRUMPET CLUB SPECIAL EDITION

JANE CUTLER

No Dogs Allowed

Pictures by
TRACEY CAMPBELL PEARSON

ISBN 0-590-42250-2

Text copyright © 1992 by Jane Cutler.
Pictures copyright © 1992 by Tracey Campbell Pearson.
All rights reserved. Published by Scholastic Inc., 555 Broadway, New York, NY 10012,
by arrangement with Farrar, Straus and Giroux, Inc.

TRUMPET and associated logos are trademarks and/or registered trademarks of
Scholastic Inc.

12 11 10 9 8 7 6 5 4 3   2 3/0

Printed in the U.S.A.   40
First Scholastic printing, February 1998

Contents

No Dogs Allowed

No Dogs

Jason and Edward Fraser wanted a dog. But their parents said they couldn't have one.

"Because you're both allergic," their mother explained. "Allergies and dogs just don't mix."

The boys walked glumly into the family room.

"I guess that's life," said Jason, who was eight.

"Rrrowf, rrrowf, grrr, ruf-ruf-ruf!" said Edward, who was almost six.

"Very funny," said Jason.

"Name Tuffles," Edward said, in a voice that sounded a little like his own voice and a little like the sort of voice a young, friendly dog might have.

"What?" asked Jason.

"Tuffles, rrrowf, *Tuffles*," replied Edward, scram-

3

bling around the family room floor on his hands and knees.

"Edward, stand up," said Jason.

Edward sat back on his heels and held his hands in front of his chest, like paws. He grinned and rolled his eyes. Then he panted: "Pant, pant!"

Jason walked away.

Edward followed, grabbing at Jason's heels.

"Quit that, Edward," Jason said.

"Rrrowf, *Tuffles*," Edward insisted.

Jason went into the back yard, and Edward followed on his hands and knees. A yellow tennis ball was on the grass. Edward tucked it under his chin and dropped it at Jason's feet.

"Edward, I want you to stop this," Jason said, picking up the ball and tossing it away.

"Ruf!" Edward retrieved the ball. "Rrowf!" he demanded, "more!"

Jason stared hard at Edward. This time he picked up the ball and put it in his pocket.

Edward kept his friendly dog eyes on Jason's face. He ducked and dodged and woofed. "Chase Tuffles," he said. "Ruf! Ruf! Chase!"

Jason tried to ignore his brother. He sat down on the back steps and studied a tiny caterpillar slowly making its way along the edge of a stair.

When he got tired of watching the caterpillar, he leaned back and watched Edward digging wildly in the flower bed, spraying the loose dirt out behind him.

For a moment, Jason thought his brother looked more like a dog digging with his paws than like a boy digging with his hands. He closed his eyes and shook his head. Then he moved into the shade of the walnut tree.

As soon as Jason settled down comfortably on the grass, Tuffles charged over, put his dirty paws on Jason's chest, and licked his face.

"That does it!" Jason sprang to his feet and started after his brother.

Tuffles made for the back door. "Mom!" he called, in his regular voice. "Mom!"

Jason grabbed Edward's T-shirt and pulled him down onto the grass. They wrestled, rolling over and over.

When they got tired, they lay on their backs, side by side, breathing hard and looking up at the blue sky, trying to find shapes and faces in the clouds.

"I see a dragon," Edward said, pointing at a dragon-shaped cloud passing overhead.

Pretty soon their noses began to run. The boys were allergic to grass, too.

———

Late Monday afternoon, when Jason came home from his friend Jeffrey's house, Edward was hard at work drawing a picture on a large piece of paper. His Magic Markers were scattered around him on the floor.

Jason stopped to look at Edward's picture. It was divided in half. The top half showed a round-faced boy with teacup ears and a scribbly patch of brown hair. The boy looked out, frowning. "Edward" was printed next to him in rambling red letters.

The bottom half of the picture showed a sleepy-looking spotted dog with a small head and big paws. The dog stood sideways. His ears hung down and his tail stuck up. "Tuffles" was printed underneath.

"Pretty good," said Jason.

"Thanks," said Edward. "Mom helped me spell."

"She helped you spell Edward?" Jason teased.

"Spell Tuffles," Edward answered.

Both boys looked at the frowning Edward and at the sideways-standing Tuffles. "You're a good artist," Jason said.

Edward nodded. He threw his arms around Jason's leg. "Ruf! Ruf!" he cried. "Me Tuffles! Ruf!"

Jason walked all the way to his bedroom with

Tuffles hanging on to one leg. Then he shook him off. "Stay," he said firmly and closed his door.

From then on, Edward was Edward about half of the time, and the other half, he was Tuffles. Jason was surprised at how good-natured his parents were about this.

"You remind me of a dog I had when I was a boy," their dad said, holding Edward on his lap and scratching him behind the ears.

"Dog food!" their mother called, setting a sandwich down at Edward's place. "Enriched with all the vitamins and minerals a growing dog needs."

"Both of you are encouraging him," Jason grumbled.

"It's only a game, honey," his mom said. "There's no harm in it."

"If Edward really thinks he's a dog, there might be harm in it," Jason pointed out. "Besides, it bugs me."

"Edward doesn't really think he's a dog, Jason," replied his mom. "Edward knows he's not a dog, doesn't he, Tuffles?" she asked, patting Edward on the head.

"Ruf!" Edward answered.

———

The next day, Edward brought his friends Emma and Betsy home after kindergarten. Jason was home already. He had a cold, so he hadn't gone to school. He was building a model airplane at the table in the kitchen.

As soon as Edward and his friends came in, they began to bark and howl and yowl. They crawled around on the kitchen floor and climbed over each other and rolled on their backs. Then Edward crawled over to Jason and put one paw in Jason's lap. "Ruf?" he said.

Jason pushed Edward's hand off his lap. "Why don't you guys play outside," he suggested. "You don't want to catch my cold."

Barking and yapping, the three kindergartners scrambled out to the yard.

"What's all that noise?" Jason's mother asked, poking her head into the kitchen.

"Edward's home," Jason answered.

"Yes?" said Mrs. Fraser.

"He brought some friends," Jason said, carefully putting together two parts of the airplane's tail. "And they're playing Humane Society."

"Humane Society?" asked his mother.

"Lonely dogs," Jason explained, "waiting to be adopted. Edward made it up, and now he and his friends play it at school."

8

"They play this game at school?" wondered Mrs. Fraser.

"Every day," Jason assured her.

"Well, then," she said, going back to the living room, where she was hanging up some new bookshelves.

The barking went on for a long time. It got louder and louder. It was so loud that Jason almost didn't hear the doorbell chime.

"Who is it?" he called as he went to the door.

"Police" was the answer.

Jason peeked out through the window next to the door. He saw a policeman and a policewoman standing there. They had on dark blue uniforms. They had badges. They had guns. Jason had on his pajamas. He felt silly, but he opened the door anyway.

"Is your mother here?" the tall policewoman asked.

"I'm here." Jason's mother came to the door, holding her drill. "Is something wrong, Officers?"

"We've had a complaint about your dogs," the short policeman said.

Mrs. Fraser looked puzzled. "We don't have dogs," she told the policeman, raising her voice so she could be heard over the sound of the barking and howling and yipping and yapping that was coming from the yard. "We don't even have *a* dog, because both of our boys are allergic."

"You don't have any dogs?" the policewoman asked.

"That's right," replied Mrs. Fraser. "We don't have dogs. We have allergies."

"Sounds like dogs to me, ma'am," said the policeman.

"Oh, that," said Mrs. Fraser.

"That's my brother and his friends," Jason explained.

Jason could tell that the officers thought he and his mother might be lying.

"Why don't we just go outside and take a look?" the policeman suggested. "Like I said, sounds like dogs to me."

"Sounds like dogs disturbing the peace, which is against the law," the policewoman pointed out.

"And it sounds like you've got more than two," added the policeman. "That's against the law in this neighborhood."

"But, Officer, only one of them is ours," said Mrs. Fraser.

"*Mom!*" Jason protested.

"There *are* dogs in the yard, then?" said the policewoman, looking shrewd, as if she'd tricked a criminal into confessing.

"What I mean is that only one of those kids out in the yard *pretending* to be a dog is ours," Mrs. Fraser said.

"Maybe we better just take a look-see, ma'am," repeated the policeman, pulling out his citation book.

Jason and his mother led the officers down the hallway and through the family room to the back yard.

As they stepped out into the yard, Mrs. Fraser pointed to the three children barking and crawling around on their hands and knees. "See?" she said, smiling. "I told you. No dogs!"

After a moment, the dogs noticed they were being watched. Two of them got the giggles and sat down on the grass, leaning back on their hands. The third one sat on his heels, held his paws up in front of his chest, and looked eager.

"See?" Mrs. Fraser said again.

The policeman folded up his citation book and put it away.

"Okay, kids," the policewoman said, "keep it down. The neighbors are complaining."

Emma and Betsy suddenly looked worried. Edward just panted playfully.

Mrs. Fraser stayed outside to talk to the children while Jason showed the officers to the front door.

"That one kid," the policeman said as they left, "he was doing a pretty convincing dog imitation, wasn't he?"

"He sure was," the policewoman said, laughing.

Jason closed the door. He felt embarrassed and angry. He went to his room and put on his clothes so he could think better. Then he sat on the couch in the family room and waited for Edward.

After his friends went home, Edward came inside.

"Edward," Jason asked, "can you imitate a lion?"

"No," Edward replied. "Can you?"

"No. How about a horse? Can you do a horse? Or an elephant? A bird? A giraffe? How about a snake?"

For a moment, Edward looked interested. But then he said, "No. Can you?"

"No," Jason admitted. "Of course I can't. It's just you're so good at dogs, I thought maybe you could do a bunch of other animals, too."

"Rrrowf," Edward said, in his Tuffles voice. "Ruf! Me Tuffles. Dog. No other animals. Ruf!"

He crawled around in circles like an excited dog chasing his own tail.

Mrs. Fraser came to the family room door. She put her finger to her lips. "Shhhh."

"Ruf!" Tuffles whispered, curling up on the rug.

"Rats!" said Jason, going back into his room to think some more.

"Rats?" asked Edward. "No. Can you?"

On the way to Dr. Bragg's for their yearly checkups, Jason sat in the front seat with his mother. Edward sat in the back, listening to a story on his Walkman.

"I think you should tell Dr. Bragg about Edward's problem," said Jason.

"Shhh," warned Mrs. Fraser.

"He can't hear me," Jason said. "He's listening to a tape."

"Oh. Then what do you mean, 'Edward's problem'?" asked Mrs. Fraser.

"You know, Mom," Jason said.

"Well, I thought I'd remind Dr. Bragg about Edward's allergies," Mrs. Fraser replied, "and about yours, too."

"Allergies are not what I'm talking about," Jason grumbled.

"Well, what are you talking about, Jason?" asked Mrs. Fraser.

Jason slid down in his seat. "I'm talking about *Tuffles*."

"Oh. Tuffles," his mother said, pulling into the parking lot at the doctor's office. She thought for a minute. "Yes, that's a good idea. I'll ask Dr. Bragg about Tuffles, too."

She turned around and took the earpieces out of Edward's ears. "We're here," she told him.

Edward turned off the tape. Then he put his front paws and his nose against the window. "Ruf!" he said. "Tuffles no like doctor."

"Mom!" Jason objected.

"Come on, boys," Mrs. Fraser said, taking their hands, "we don't want to be late for our appointment."

Behind his mother's back, Edward gave Jason a mischievous Tuffles look, rolling his eyes and holding his head to one side like a curious pup. Jason looked away, pretending not to notice.

Dr. Bragg's waiting room was crowded, as usual. Jason looked at a magazine. Edward watched a goldfish swimming around in its bowl.

After a long time, Dr. Bragg's nurse opened the door. "Frasers? Come on in!" she called.

"Finally," Jason muttered.

"Ruf!" Edward agreed.

"Don't start that," Jason warned.

First it was Jason's turn. Edward and Mrs. Fraser watched while Dr. Bragg put his cold stethoscope up against Jason's chest. "Take deep breaths, Jason," the doctor said. "Cough. Breathe naturally. Now pant."

Jason hesitated. He glanced at Edward. Edward was sitting on the edge of his chair, looking eager. Jason frowned at him.

"Pant, Jason," Dr. Bragg repeated.

"I'll show you how, Jason," Edward said, wriggling off his chair and smiling. He stood next to the examining table. He let his eyes roll up. He let his tongue hang out. "Pant-pant-pant-pant-rrrrowff! Pant-pant!"

Jason closed his eyes and grimaced.

"Pretty good," said Dr. Bragg, smiling. "Now you do it, Jason."

Jason panted. Once. "Again?" said Dr. Bragg.

"Jason, like *this*," said Edward. "Pant-pant-pant-pant." He stopped, looking pleased with himself, like a small dog waiting for a pat on the head.

Dr. Bragg laughed.

"Pant," went Jason.

"Their allergies?" Mrs. Fraser asked Dr. Bragg at the end of the examinations.

"Something they just have to live with," Dr. Bragg told her.

"And the dog imitation?" Mrs. Fraser inquired.

"One of the best I've seen," the doctor said.

———

"Summer vacation will be here in three months," Mr. Fraser told Jason and Edward one evening. "It's time for the two of you to learn how to swim."

"Not again!" objected Jason.

"Again," his father told him firmly.

"But we don't even like to play in the water," Jason reminded his father.

"I know," Mr. Fraser said.

"Last summer, when you tried to teach us to swim, the water made our noses run," complained Edward.

"I remember," said Mr. Fraser. "But it's time you boys knew how to swim anyway. It's a matter of safety. So I've signed you up at the Y for real swimming lessons."

"*Drowning* lessons," muttered Jason, remembering last year's thrashing and splashing.

"Ruf! *Drowning*," Tuffles agreed.

Jason tried reasoning with his mother. "We're perfectly safe without knowing how to swim."

"Oh, I don't know about that," she said. "Everyone needs to learn to swim, just in case."

"Just in case what?" Jason asked.

"Well, just in case you fall out of a boat and have to swim to shore," his mother said. "For example."

"We never go in boats," said Jason.

"You might," his mother said.

"We wouldn't if we didn't know how to swim," said Jason. "It would be too dangerous."

"Exactly!" said his mother.

"Tuffles no like water," Edward grumbled. "Tuffles no like swim."

"Good," said Mrs. Fraser, "because the swimming pool is no place for a dog."

"Ruf?" asked Edward.

"That's right," Mrs. Fraser said. "No dogs allowed at the pool."

Jason felt a little better. At least he wouldn't have to worry about Tuffles at the same time he was trying to learn to swim. Or would he? He looked long and hard at Edward, who was begging for a cookie exactly the way a pup begs for a dog biscuit.

There would be ten lessons. Jason and Edward slowly got ready for the first one. They put on their bathing suits and their sweats. They rolled up their towels and tucked them under their arms. They slipped their feet into rubber flip-flops. Reluctantly, they climbed into the back seat of the car.

"Cheer up," their mother suggested.

"Ruf," said Tuffles.

"No dogs allowed, remember?" Jason said, poking Edward with his elbow.

"Rrrowf!" answered Edward, poking back.

"Just don't make this any worse than it already is, Edward Fraser," Jason warned.

"You don't need to talk to Edward that way, Jason," Mrs. Fraser said. "He knows Tuffles stays in the car."

"Ruf," said Edward, putting his arms around his towel and looking out the window.

The indoor pool was long and narrow. The water smelled of chemicals. Jason and Edward sat on a bench at the shallow end with the other beginners. They were all called Tadpoles.

"Hi there, Tadpoles," the swimming teacher said cheerfully. "I'm Maggie, and I'm going to help you learn how to swim."

Maggie wore a red bathing suit. She had a whistle around her neck, and she was holding a clipboard and a pen.

"First, I need you to tell me your names," she said. "Your full names, please, and I'll write them down on my list. Then we'll get into the water. Today, we're going to learn the dead man's float. And in a couple of weeks, I bet all you Tadpoles will be ready to learn how to dog-paddle."

Dog-paddle! Jason was afraid to look at Edward.

Dog-paddle! It was practically an invitation.

Maggie was moving down the line of children, taking names. It was almost Jason's turn. Then it would be Edward's.

Dog-paddle! Jason sneaked a look at Edward. Edward had that eager Tuffles expression on his face.

"Edward, *no!*" Jason whispered fiercely.

Edward put his hands up in front of his chest, like paws, and rolled his eyes.

"And what's your name?" Maggie asked Jason.

"Jason Fraser," he said unhappily, glaring at his brother.

"Okay, Jason, nice to meet you," Maggie said, writing down his name.

"And yours?" she said to Edward.

Jason closed his eyes and hunched his shoulders. He waited for the sound of panting. He waited for a little bark. He waited for that Tuffles voice.

"Your name?" Maggie asked again, waiting patiently for Edward to answer her.

"Christopher Fishman," said Edward, in his Edward voice.

Jason opened his eyes and stared at Edward. Edward, looking calm, looking nothing like Tuffles, kept his eyes on the teacher as she wrote down the name.

"Okay, Tadpoles," she called when she finished writing, "into the water now."

Holding on to the side of the pool, Jason and Edward slid into the warm, shallow water. *"Christopher Fishman?"* Jason asked as his feet touched the bottom and his bathing suit ballooned around his legs.

"You can call me Chris," said Edward pleasantly. "Chris Fish." Then he opened his eyes very wide, sucked in his cheeks, made kissing movements with his mouth, and gracefully waved his hands back and forth in the water, like fins.

Rideout and Gateway

On Friday, Jason and Edward brought home a wagonload of books from the library. Mrs. Fraser watched with interest as they carried the books into the house and set them in neat stacks on the floor in Jason's room.

"Looks as if you two have practically cleaned out the Children's Room," said Mrs. Fraser. "What's up?"

"Look-at-a-Book Week at our school," Jason told her.

"Whoever reads the most books this week and does the best special book project will win a surprise," said Edward.

"A *prize*," corrected Jason.

"So we're going to cooperate and try to win," finished Edward.

"Is that fair?" asked Mrs. Fraser.

"Is what fair?" said Edward.

"To cooperate? In a contest?"

"Cooperating between students is encouraged, but not required," said Jason, making his voice sound like his teacher's.

"We're going to cooperate a lot," said Edward. "We have to, since I can't really read yet."

"That makes sense," said Mrs. Fraser.

"We're cooperating already," Edward explained. "We took turns pulling the wagon."

Jason and Edward went into Jason's bedroom and sat down on the floor with the books. They decided to organize them. They separated the small books from the large ones. They separated the books about animals from the books about people. They put the books with a lot of pictures on one pile, and they put the books with not so many pictures on another pile.

When they got tired of organizing the books, they began to build things with them. They made tents by setting the books open on the floor, spines up. They made a tent city and ran their pocket cars around in it. Then they carefully made two bridges out of books and ran the cars back and forth over and under them.

After that, Jason started to read a book about a dinosaur, and Edward started looking at a book about a cat who wore boots, and they both lay contentedly on the floor until Mr. Fraser got home from work and Mrs. Fraser called them to supper.

Jason and Edward knew if they wanted to win the prize, they would have to come up with an outstanding idea for a special project. They decided to make a book of their own.

On Saturday morning, they got to work.

"Edward will do the pictures," Jason explained to his mother. "He can draw."

"And Jason will do the story," Edward told her. "He can read and write."

"Sounds like a good way to divide up the work," said Mrs. Fraser, helping the boys set themselves up in the book-making business, one at each end of the dining room table.

At his end, Edward had a plastic cloth to protect the table. He had a stack of different-colored construction paper. He had Magic Markers and a jumbo box of crayons and a package of colored chalk. He had a new eraser. He had watercolor paints and two brushes and a jelly jar half-full of water. He had scissors and a hole puncher and a glue stick. He had a stamp pad and an assortment of stamps. He had a stapler. He had tape.

At his end, Jason had a piece of lined paper and a pencil.

Edward sighed happily as he chose a sheet of pale blue construction paper and set it down squarely in front of him. He smiled to himself and hummed under his breath as he carefully arranged all of his art supplies neatly around the sheet of paper. He made sure he could reach everything, and that nothing was in anything else's way. Then he picked up a Magic Marker.

Jason watched Edward. "What do you think you're doing?" he asked grumpily.

Edward looked up, surprised at Jason's surly tone. "I'm getting ready to draw a picture," he said, "like I'm supposed to. For our book. That you're going to write."

"Not yet," Jason said.

Edward put down his Magic Marker.

Jason frowned at his sheet of paper and put the eraser end of his pencil up against his lips.

Edward picked up the marker.

"I said not yet," said Jason.

"Why not?" Edward asked.

"Because the writing has to come first."

26

"Why?"

"Because that's the way they do it," Jason told him impatiently. "My teacher said so. First they write the words. Then they draw the pictures."

"Why?" asked Edward.

"How should I know?" Jason shouted.

Edward sighed again, in frustration. "Then hurry up and write so I can start to draw," he said.

"I can't hurry up," Jason said angrily. "It isn't so easy to write a story. It takes time. It takes thought. It takes concentration. Sometimes you have to write it over and over again until you get it right. You don't just sit down and write a story. You have to think about it. It's a very hard thing to do."

Edward considered this. "So when do I get to draw the pictures?"

"I told you, not until after I finish."

"If it's such a hard thing to do, you might never finish," Edward said, looking sadly at the art supplies arranged neatly on the table in front of him.

"Too bad for you, then," said Jason. "Now be quiet so I can think."

"Too bad for you, too, then," said Edward, picking up his Magic Marker again and beginning to work on a picture he'd thought of while he and Jason were arguing.

"I—said—wait!" Jason commanded.

"I said NO!" Edward hollered.

By the time Mrs. Fraser came to see what the fuss was about, the boys had rolled under the table and Jason was on top of Edward. "Boys!" she cried, crawling under the table to separate them.

Mrs. Fraser held Jason with her right hand. She held Edward with her left. "What in the world is going on here?" she asked. "Is this what you two call cooperation?"

"He says I can't make the pictures until he writes the dumb story," cried Edward indignantly. "And it might take him a hundred years to write it!"

"Is that true, Jason?" Mrs. Fraser asked.

Jason didn't answer. He wrapped his arms around his knees and looked away from his mother.

Edward wrapped his arms around his knees and looked away from his mother, too. In the other direction.

Mrs. Fraser sat cross-legged and hunched over, so as not to hit her head on the bottom of the table-top.

"Is that true, Jason?" she asked again.

"Not really."

"Not really?"

"Not exactly."

"Not exactly?"

"All I said was, the story comes first, and then

you make the pictures to go with it. So he has to wait."

"And just sit there, for the rest of my life!" said Edward.

"Yeah, just sit there with all your markers and your crayons and your scissors and your tape and your glue and your stapler and your stamp pad and . . . everything. While I have to write a whole story on just one piece of paper. With a pencil."

"I see," said Mrs. Fraser. "Well."

She crawled out from underneath the table. So did the boys. Jason went back to his end of the table. Edward went back to his.

"You think it might be more fun to do the pictures than to write the story," Mrs. Fraser said to Jason.

Jason looked down.

"You wish you had a bunch of stuff to work with, like Edward does."

Jason nodded.

"But you're the writer, not the artist, so you don't have much stuff to work with."

Jason nodded.

"All you've got is a pencil and a piece of paper," she said. Then she added, "And whatever's in your head, of course."

Jason looked at her suspiciously.

"Anyway, why don't you begin your story and tell Edward what it's about, and he can start on the pictures while you do the writing. In the end, it'll probably work out just fine, don't you think?"

"I think it will," said Edward cheerfully, picking up his Magic Marker once more. "What is the story going to be about, Jason?" he asked, holding the marker ready over the paper.

Jason thought. "The story," he said, "is going to be about a very poor boy who doesn't have any toys but is a fast runner and has a lot of friends . . ."

Edward nodded happily and began to draw a picture of the boy, running fast.

"And this poor boy meets a very rich boy, who has a lot of stuff to play with, but who is a very slow runner and has no friends at all."

"And they get to be friends," Edward said, busily drawing. "And the poor boy shows the rich boy how to run faster and teaches him how to make friends. And the rich boy shares all his toys with the poor boy. Right, Jason?"

"No!" said Jason.

"Well, what, then?" asked Edward.

"I don't know yet," said Jason, starting to write. "But not that."

31

Once he got started, Jason worked quickly. This is what he wrote:

THERE WAS A BOY WHO WAS A FAST RUNNER. HE HAD A LOT OF FRIENDS. HE LIKED TO READ STORIES. HE LIKED TO LISTEN TO STORIES. BUT HE DID NOT LIKE TO WRITE THEM.
                    THE END

When he finished writing his story, Jason went outside and practiced running back and forth in the driveway. "On your mark, get set, go!" he cried, and off he went as fast as he could.

Drawing a picture of a boy running didn't really interest Edward. It wasn't what he wanted to draw. So after Jason went outside to run up and down in the driveway, Edward put that picture aside and drew a different one. He drew a torpedo-shaped orange ship sailing on wavy blue water. Then he drew a deep-sea diver and cut him out and pasted him down in the water under the ship. Then he drew some very large fish and cut them out and pasted them down in the water, too. After that, he went outside and took over the ready-set-go! part for Jason.

———

On Friday morning, all the lower-school classes assembled in the multipurpose room. It was the day the prize would be awarded. What's more, a children's book illustrator and a children's book writer were going to visit. The first, second, and third graders sat in rows on folding chairs. The kindergartners sat on the floor in the front. The principal, Ms. Wilkinson, was there, and the teachers, and the aides, and Mr. Farrell, the school librarian. The place was packed.

Jason sat with the other third graders about halfway back. He could see Edward right up front, sitting cross-legged on the floor with the rest of the kindergartners. Jason noticed how much smaller the kindergarten kids were than they had been when he was in kindergarten. "Those kids get littler every year," he said to Andrea Peterson, who was sitting next to him.

"What kids?" Andrea asked.

"The kindergarten kids," Jason explained, frowning. "Last year they were smaller. And this year they're even smaller. If they keep getting smaller and smaller every year, pretty soon they'll be little enough to keep in your pocket."

Andrea stared at Jason and didn't answer. He slumped down in his chair, brooding. He and Edward hadn't read very many books, and they hadn't finished a special project, either. There was no chance they would win the prize.

Up front, on one side of the raised platform, was a large easel with a giant pad of drawing paper on it. On the other side of the platform were a small, square table and a straight-backed chair.

First, Ms. Wilkinson welcomed everyone. She reminded the children about manners and the way they were supposed to act when guests were kind enough to visit. She hoped, she said, looking firmly from one kindergarten child to the next, that everyone would be extremely polite and pay attention and keep their hands to themselves.

Now, she said, she would have the pleasure of awarding the prize to the student who had done the most outstanding job of participating in Look-at-a-Book Week. Then she would turn the program over to the guests.

"The prize for outstanding effort and achievement goes to Lucas Lawrence Larraby," Ms. Wilkinson announced, smiling. "Please come up front, Lucas," she said, "and get your prize."

Lucas, a tall third grader, stood up. His friend Arnie Pollock, who was sitting next to him, socked him in the arm. Lucas stopped to sock Arnie back. "Up front now, please, Lucas," Ms. Wilkinson said, still smiling.

Mr. Fortney, the third-grade teacher, put his hand on Lucas's back and set him on his course toward the front of the room.

"We are very proud of you, Lucas," Ms. Wilkinson said as the boy shambled up to the platform. "You have read *twelve* books in only one week and, what's more, you have written and illustrated this —ah—this *imaginative* book of your own!"

Ms. Wilkinson held up a large, handmade book so the rest of the children could see it. The picture on the cover showed two monsters crawling out of a computer screen. The title, in bold black letters, said: THE WRONG PROGRAM.

"Way to go, Lucas!" Arnie Pollock called out.

Mr. Fortney eyeballed Arnie.

"So, for your outstanding effort and accomplishment," Ms. Wilkinson said to Lucas, "I am very pleased to award you the prize: a gift certificate for twenty dollars from Colby's Children's Bookstore."

Lucas looked down at the floor and said thank you so quietly that only the kindergartners could hear him. Then he shook hands with the principal, took his gift certificate and his book, and started back to his seat. The students clapped and several of them called out, "Lucas, can I read your book?"

"It's time now," Ms. Wilkinson said, holding up

her hands for order, "to turn the program over to Mr. Warren Rideout, children's book illustrator, and Mr. Garson Gateway, children's book writer."

The illustrator, a big, bald man, wearing cowboy boots and a bolo necktie, clomped to the easel and noisily pulled it to the center of the platform. The author, a thin young man, wearing a brown suit and a brown knitted vest, slipped into the straight-backed chair and put some books down on the small table.

"I'll go first," said the illustrator, Mr. Rideout, and he began energetically to talk and to draw at the same time.

Before their eyes, the children saw all sorts of pictures appear on the large pad of paper on the easel. The artist spoke quickly and drew quickly. Soon the whole room vibrated with laughter and excitement. And when Mr. Rideout finished and wiped the sweat off his bald head with a large red handkerchief, everyone begged for more. Mr. Rideout clasped his hands over his head, the way a winner does, and clomped back to his seat next to Ms. Wilkinson.

Then it was Garson Gateway's turn. The writer sat with his hands on his knees and looked shyly out at the children.

"Well," he said, nodding toward the books on

the table next to him. "Here are some of the books I've written. They're not picture books," he said. "But they do have some pictures in them." He held up a book opened to a page that had a black-and-white picture on it. "And they have pictures on the jackets," he said, holding up two more books so that the children could see the art on the covers.

"My books," he said again. "Perhaps some of you have read them?"

There was silence. The writer seemed sad. "In any case," he said, "I have written them." He waited. "Are there any questions?"

Nobody but Jason raised a hand. "How do you write?" Jason asked.

"I write slowly," answered Garson Gateway.

"I think Jason means what do you use to write with," Ms. Wilkinson said. "Is that correct, Jason?"

Jason nodded.

"Oh," said the writer. "Well, I write on a word processor. And if I get stuck, then I write on my typewriter. And if that doesn't work, then I write with a pencil on a piece of paper."

"What if you're still stuck?" called out Arnie Pollock.

"Then I run around my house. Outside, I mean," admitted the writer.

Edward raised his hand. "Can you write something for us?" he asked.

The writer looked apologetic. "No, I'm afraid I can't. I mean, I could write my name and address or something like that. But I couldn't write a story. Not right here in front of you. Not the way Mr. Rideout can draw pictures."

"Why not?" asked Edward.

"Writing a story is different from drawing pictures," Mr. Gateway explained. "It's, well, it's an interesting thing to *do,* but it's not very interesting to *watch* someone do."

The writer looked at the children's disappointed faces. "I could *read* you something from a book I've already written," he suggested hopefully.

Jason raised his hand again. "Where do you get the ideas for your stories," Jason asked, "before you write them down?"

"I get them out of my head," the writer answered. "My head is full of stories. Isn't yours?"

"Yes, mine is," Jason said.

"So's mine," said Arnie Pollock. "But I don't like the writing-down part. It's too hard."

"And I don't like the writing-down part, too," said Edward, sitting up on his knees, "because I don't know how to write yet."

"Me too," said Emily Han, who was sitting next to Edward.

"What you're saying is, you all have stories in your heads, just like I do, right?" said Mr. Gateway, leaning forward in his chair.

"Right," several students called out.

"But you don't write them down, because it's hard to get what's in your head down on paper, right?"

"Right," more students agreed.

"But if you could say your stories out loud," Mr. Gateway suggested, "which isn't so very different from writing them down—after all, stories were told out loud for thousands of years before anyone wrote them down—you'd be able to tell your stories. Right?"

"Right!" shouted almost everyone.

"Well," said Garson Gateway thoughtfully, "we could write a story out loud, together. Here. Now. And maybe Mr. Rideout would be kind enough to illustrate it for us as we go along. Shall we try?"

Ms. Wilkinson came forward quickly. "That's very generous of you, Mr. Gateway. How many of you children would like to hear Mr. Gateway *tell* you a story, since you can't actually see him write one?"

Mr. Gateway stood up. "Not *me* tell a story," he

corrected the principal. "*All* of us tell one. Together."

"Yes, of course," the principal said, "together." She leaned toward Mr. Gateway. "A recipe for disaster," she whispered. Then she turned to the children. "How many of you would like to try to write a story out loud, together, with Mr. Gateway?"

Almost every hand went up.

Ms. Wilkinson beamed at the writer. "It's your funeral," she said to him, so quietly that only a few of the kindergartners sitting at the very front could hear her.

"Well," Mr. Gateway said, "let's give it a try."

Mr. Rideout got up and stood gamely at the easel. "I'm ready," he said.

"All right, then, here we go," Mr. Gateway said. "Once upon a time, there was . . ."

"A funeral!" Edward called out cheerfully—he had heard Ms. Wilkinson.

"A tall, strong girl," called out Juana Gomez from the back row.

"Once upon a time," said Mr. Gateway, "there was a tall, strong girl who lived . . ."

"On a houseboat by herself!" said Jeremy Lustig.

The writer nodded at Jeremy. "And who had to . . ." he said.

"Make her own way in the world, since her parents had been kidnapped!" called out Mr. Fortney, looking surprised at himself.

Soon they were all busy making up the story, which was a mystery-adventure that included stolen treasure and pirates and storms and magic and got more exciting by the minute while Mr. Rideout frantically drew one picture after another as fast as he could, showing all the different characters and the amazing things that were happening to them.

When the story was finally finished, the tall, strong girl, whose name was Esmeralda, was setting out once again in her flimsy houseboat onto the wide, winding, treacherous river that ran right past her door, ready to have even more adventures, as soon as someone could think them up.

But for the moment, the writers were exhausted, and their heads felt as empty as balloons. What they needed, they all agreed, was a run around the soccer field and then some lunch.

Killer Kelly

Edward heard about the new boy before he ever saw him. The boy's name was Andrew Kelly, he lived in what used to be the Hendersons' house, and he was the biggest kid in the fourth grade.

"He's enormous," Jason said.

"Humongous," agreed Jason's friend Morley, who was visiting after school.

"Killer Kelly," Jason joked nervously.

"How big is he?" Edward asked. "Is he bigger than Dad?"

"Of course he's not bigger than Dad," said Jason. "He's a fourth grader."

"He's not bigger than your dad," Morley agreed. "But he's a lot bigger than we are."

"And a lot meaner, too," said Jason, taking out bread, peanut butter, milk, and chocolate chips.

"Are you sure about that?" Edward asked.

"Sure about what?" said Jason.

"Are you sure he's meaner than you are?"

Morley and Jason both glared at Edward.

"Put a lot of chocolate chips on my sandwich," Edward reminded Jason.

"Fix your own sandwich," Jason said. "These are for Morley and me."

"So what makes you think he's meaner?" Edward said pointedly.

"Because he does stuff we'd never do," Morley said.

"He does stuff we'd never even think about doing," Jason said.

"Like what stuff?" asked Edward.

"Like, he fries ants with a magnifying glass," Morley said, pouring out two glasses of milk.

"He focuses the sun right on them, on the ants, until they sizzle and pop!" explained Jason, spreading peanut butter on four pieces of bread and sprinkling the chocolate chips on top of the peanut butter.

"And if you look at him wrong, he beats you up right then and there," added Morley. "He knows how to sock you so it really hurts, because he has

44

three older brothers and they've been socking him all his life. That's how he learned."

"What do you mean, look at him *wrong*?" asked Edward.

"At all," answered Jason. "He doesn't like being looked at."

"Probably because he looks like an elephant," said Morley.

"And a hippopotamus," said Jason.

"And a rhinoceros," said Morley.

"And a *brontosaurus*," said Jason.

The two boys picked up their milk and their peanut-butter-and-chocolate-chip sandwiches and headed for Jason's room.

"And if he gets really mad at you," Jason called back over his shoulder to Edward, "he cuts the brake line on your bike!"

Edward was just learning to ride his two-wheeler. "So how can you stop your bike, then?" he called after Jason.

"The only way you *can* stop without brakes, dumbo," Jason replied. "You fall over!"

Morley and Jason disappeared into Jason's room, laughing in what Edward considered a mean way. Edward made himself a chocolate-chip sandwich without peanut butter and poured himself a glass of milk. When his mother came in to fix herself a snack, he said, "Did you hear about the new kid?"

"What new kid?" she asked.

"Andrew Kelly. He's a fourth grader. He lives where the Hendersons used to live."

"Right around the corner," Mrs. Fraser said. "That's nice."

"It's not nice. He's mean."

"Mean?" his mother asked, rummaging in the refrigerator as if she was sure there must be something in there she wanted, if only she could find it.

"Really mean. Meaner than Jason," Edward muttered.

Mrs. Fraser came out of the refrigerator looking disappointed, with a carrot in one hand and a piece of celery in the other. "Meaner than Jason? Wow. Pretty mean, I'd say."

Edward knew she was teasing him. She didn't think Jason was mean.

"Do you know what he does?"

"What Jason does?"

"What Andrew Kelly does."

"What?"

"He *fries* ants."

"Fries ants?" she said, clearly interested.

"Until they *sizzle* and *pop*," Edward said, watching her carefully.

"We used to do that," Mrs. Fraser said. "You

need a magnifying glass to focus the sun through. Then you need to hold it steady, while the dot of sunlight focused through the lens heats up. Usually, when it starts getting hot, the ants run away. You have to lasso them and throw them down on the ground to get them to stay put, so you can fry them."

"Lasso the ants?" Edward asked.

"Yep," his mother said, crunching down on her carrot and leaving the kitchen. "At least, that's the way we did it when I was a kid. Might be different now."

Edward got the big magnifying glass out of the top drawer of his father's desk. As far as he could remember, no one had ever told him he couldn't use it. Then he went outside.

Squatting in the driveway, he practiced catching the light of the sun and focusing it. That part was easy. He duck-walked around the driveway, focusing the sunlight and looking for ants. Occasionally he saw one. Usually it was carrying something larger than itself. Or it was telling a secret to an ant it had met going in the opposite direction.

The ants were busy. Edward doubted any of them would stay still long enough for him to focus the sun on them and heat them up until they popped. He wondered how you got ants to do that. Maybe you did it to pet ants, he thought, ants you'd trained to hold still. But who would want to sizzle a trained pet ant? Now he wished he'd asked his mother exactly *how* she used to lasso ants.

Edward put the magnifying glass back in his father's drawer. If he ever met this Andrew, and if he managed to catch him in a good mood, he'd ask him how to do it. Maybe he could even get Andrew to show him. Edward thought happily about that for a few minutes, imagining himself and Andrew squatting side by side, frying ants together. That would give old Jason something to think about.

Edward decided to check his bike, which he'd left in the driveway. He looked at the tires and the spokes and the brake line and the chain. Everything seemed all right. Then he decided to take a walk around the block, to see if anything interesting was happening.

First he went by Alexander Friedman's house. Alexander was a second grader who wasn't at all mean and who would play with just about anyone.

Edward got to Alexander's just in time to see Alexander tear around the corner of the house, running as fast as he could run, with his arms pumping at his sides. A few feet behind him was

Mrs. Friedman, his mother, wearing a pink warm-up suit and one pink bedroom slipper, and waving the other one in the air as she ran after him. Edward stopped to watch. Over the fence into the back yard went Alexander, who was remarkably athletic. Over the fence, right on his heels, went Mrs. Friedman, crying, "Think you can get away from me that easily? Never!"

Neither one of the Friedmans noticed Edward, so he walked on.

He saw that the Conroy kids had some sort of stand set up in front of their house. Maybe lemonade, he thought hopefully.

When he got closer, he saw it wasn't lemonade. It was tooth-pulling. Marlene and Marilyn Conroy wanted to pull teeth for people. But they had no customers.

"Only twenty-five cents a tooth," Marlene told Edward.

"Quick and painless," Marilyn added.

"No lemonade?" Edward asked.

"Not today," Marlene said. "Today we're doing teeth. Yesterday we cut hair. You could use a haircut. You should have been here yesterday."

"That was yesterday, Marlene," Marilyn interrupted. "Today it's teeth."

"I don't have any money," Edward told them.

"Well," Marlene said, "do you have any loose teeth?"

Edward thought. He did have loose teeth. Two of them. "No," he said.

"Are you sure?" Marlene asked.

"We might do it for nothing," Marilyn offered.

"I'm pretty sure," said Edward. "Nothing loose enough to pull out."

Both girls stepped forward.

"Not today. Maybe next time," Edward said, backing quickly away. " 'Bye!"

Edward saw a teenager go past on a bike, riding no-hands and carrying a basketball.

He saw another teenager go past in the other direction on a bike, riding no-hands and carrying a pot of tulips.

He thought about riding no-hands. He wondered how people did it. He wondered if Andrew Kelly could ride no-hands. He wondered if Andrew Kelly pulled out his own teeth when they were loose. He wondered how it would feel to be walking along the street and to be Andrew Kelly.

Edward began to walk the way he thought Andrew Kelly would walk. He took long, firm steps. He shoved his hands into his front pockets. He pushed his head forward. He squinted meanly and sneered.

51

Edward could tell he looked just like Killer Kelly. He could feel it.

"Hi, Edward," said Mrs. Yamamoto, who was outside watering.

Edward wondered how she recognized him.

"Hi," he answered. Then he ran the rest of the way down the block to the corner.

As he ran, he pretended that Andrew Kelly was chasing him, the way Mrs. Friedman had been chasing Alexander. Instead of waving a bedroom slipper, Andrew Kelly was waving a pair of pliers. He had heard about Edward's loose teeth. He was going to snatch them right out of Edward's mouth. That's how mean he was.

Edward ran as fast as he could. He could hear Andrew Kelly's footsteps behind him, getting closer and closer. He knew he could never outrun the biggest fourth grader in the school. If he could only get to the tall, tangled old bushes around the corner at the end of the block, he could duck into the middle of them and hide. When Andrew Kelly came by, he would just look around and scratch his head. Edward would have disappeared. No one knew about the hiding place in the bushes except Edward and Jason. It was one of their secret hideouts.

Edward skidded around the corner and dove for

cover, sliding into the empty place he and Jason had cleared out in the middle of the bushes. He lay on his side and stayed perfectly still with his eyes closed, breathing hard and listening, until he heard Andrew's clodhoppers going right on by.

He'd done it. He'd fooled Killer Kelly. He'd gotten away. He was safe.

Edward opened his eyes and sat up, wiping the sweat off his face with his shirtsleeve and breathing in the nice green and dusty smell of the secret hiding place.

It was then that he saw another kid sitting there, staring at him. A big kid. A kid Edward had never seen before.

"Hi," Edward said. "You're in our secret hiding place."

"Whose secret hiding place?" asked the stranger.

"My brother Jason's and mine," Edward answered.

"I just found it," the kid explained. "I didn't know it belonged to anybody."

"Oh, it doesn't really," Edward said. "We just pretend it's ours. And use it. And don't tell anyone. You know."

The big kid nodded. "So who was chasing you?" he asked.

Edward looked around, to make sure no one else

could hear. He looked serious. He lowered his voice. "Andrew Kelly," he said.

The other boy was interested. "Andrew Kelly?" he asked. "Really?"

"Yeah," Edward bragged. "He's the meanest kid in our school and he's been chasing me all around the neighborhood, trying to pull out my loose teeth with pliers. But I tricked him." Edward lay back with his arms folded under his head. "And I ran faster than he did, too."

"You outran and outsmarted Andrew Kelly," the big kid said, scooting closer to Edward, putting his face right down to Edward's, and staring squarely into Edward's eyes.

Edward stared back. He wished the big kid would move away a little and not put his face so close.

"What do you think Andrew Kelly would've done to you if he'd caught you—what's your name?" the big kid asked.

"Edward," Edward said in a small voice. "What's yours?"

"What do you think Kelly would have done to you if he'd caught you, *Edward*?" the boy said.

"I think he would have—um—made friends with me," Edward lied. "And—um—I think he would have—shown me how to fry ants with a magnifying glass!"

"What about the pliers?" the boy asked, not moving away even a quarter of an inch.

"Oh, that was just a joke," Edward said. "It was just—a joke."

"The pliers were a joke?" the boy asked, squinting down at Edward.

"It was all a joke!" Edward cried, suddenly rolling over and scrambling to his feet. "It was all just a joke. I made it up. Nobody was chasing me. Honest. I was only playing."

"I know that," the boy said. He sat cross-legged on the ground, picked up a stick, and started peeling off the bark. "I knew that all along."

"You knew?" Edward asked, squatting down and picking up a stick of his own. "How'd you know?"

The boy tossed his stick away. "How do you think?" he asked impatiently. He stood up, thrust his head forward, and glared down at Edward. "How do you think I knew?" he repeated.

Edward looked up at the big new kid towering over him. Then he looked down and started drawing in the dirt with his stick. He shrugged and pretended to be very interested in what he was drawing.

"What do you think my name is?" the boy demanded.

"Joe?" guessed Edward.

"Not *Joe!*" the boy yelled.

"Moe?" said Edward.

"Not *Moe!*" the boy hollered.

"Rumpelstiltskin?" asked Edward, cracking himself up.

"Rumpelstiltskin?" asked the boy. "NO!" he roared.

"Well, what is your name, then?" said Edward, keeping his head down so the big kid wouldn't see him laughing.

"My name is ANDREW KELLY!" the kid yelled, stamping his feet in frustration.

"I knew that," Edward said, standing up again and tossing his stick away. "Do you fry ants with a magnifying glass?"

Killer Kelly looked sideways at Edward. "Maybe," he said.

"Do you sock anyone who looks at you?" Edward asked.

"You've been looking at me," Killer Kelly replied. "Have I socked you?"

"If you got mad at someone, would you cut the brake line on his bike?" Edward asked.

"Of course not!" Killer Kelly said. "Why would I do a thing like that?"

"So what makes you so mean and bad?" Edward asked.

"Who says I am?"

"Everybody."

"Who's everybody?"

"Oh, just some kids I know," Edward said.

"They always say that when I go to a new school. Because I'm big. People think you're mean and bad if you're bigger than everybody else. They like to think so."

"Why?" asked Edward.

Andrew Kelly shrugged. "They get over it, though, when they get to know you."

"What happens until they get to know you and get over it?" Edward asked.

"You have to fool around by yourself," said Andrew.

"What do you do, fooling around by yourself?"

"Oh, I ride my bike and my skateboard," said Andrew, "and I practice shooting baskets. Sometimes I read. And I collect insects."

"What kind of insects?"

"Just about any kind I can find. Centipedes and millipedes and spiders and earwigs and tarantulas, sometimes. That's what I was doing here, actually, when you slid in. I was looking for insects for my collection."

Edward stared at the ground. He didn't see any insects. "Where were you looking?"

"Underneath rocks. That's where they are, mostly. See?" Andrew Kelly picked up a medium-sized, grayish rock. He and Edward both examined the ground underneath it.

"Nothing," Edward said.

"Are you sure?" asked Andrew.

Edward pointed to the empty space on the ground where the rock had been. "Nothing there," he said.

"You forgot something," Andrew said.

"What?"

"You forgot to look underneath the *rock*."

Andrew turned over the rock he was holding, and Edward saw three sow bugs scurrying around on the bottom of it. Andrew put it down again. "I don't collect sow bugs. That's too easy."

"Yeah," said Edward. "I don't, either."

Edward and Andrew turned over a bunch of rocks. But all they found was sow bugs. "This hiding place isn't a very good collecting place," Andrew said.

"It's not even a very good hiding place," Edward observed.

"Well, it's better than some," said Andrew.

"Do you ever fry ants with a magnifying glass?" Edward asked again.

"Sometimes," Andrew allowed. "Why?"

"Well, I just wondered how you do it. When I tried, the ants were busy, and they wouldn't stay still. My mom said when she was a kid, she used to have to lasso them."

"Lasso them?" Andrew said. "That's interesting. I wonder how she did that?"

"We could ask her," Edward suggested. "Or you could just show me how you do it yourself."

"Where do you live?" Andrew asked.

"Around the corner," Edward said.

"Let's go," said Andrew.

They crawled out of the secret hiding place and started to walk to Edward's. Edward watched to see how Andrew Kelly walked, so he could walk the same way.

Andrew thrust his hands deep down into his pockets. So did Edward. Andrew took long, smooth steps. So did Edward. Andrew stood tall and held his head up proudly. So did Edward.

By the time they got to Edward's house, Edward had the hang of it. He could walk exactly like Andrew Kelly. He knew how it felt to walk around being the tallest kid in the fourth grade and having everyone in the neighborhood afraid of you, whether they needed to be or not.

Andrew waited in the driveway while Edward went inside and got his father's magnifying glass again. Jason and Morley were in Jason's room, making paper airplanes.

Edward stopped at Jason's door. "Hi," he said cheerfully.

"We're busy," said Jason.

"I'm going outside to fry some ants," Edward said.

"Sure," said Morley.

"With my new friend that I just met," continued Edward. "He's going to show me how. He does it all the time."

Jason and Morley ignored Edward.

"Well, I'm going now," Edward said. "Outside. To fry ants with Andrew Kelly."

Jason and Morley looked at each other. Then they followed Edward to the front door and looked out into the driveway, where Andrew Kelly was waiting.

"That's Andrew Kelly!" exclaimed Jason.

"That's what I told you," sang Edward.

The look on Jason's face was very satisfying to Edward. He grinned over his shoulder at his brother as he went on outside.

Four Eyes, Three Heads

Jason and Edward sat in the kitchen. Jason was reading, with his chin resting on the table. His nose was two inches away from his book. Edward was drawing, with *his* chin resting on the table. *His* nose was two inches away from his picture.

Mrs. Fraser poked her head into the kitchen. "Not so close, boys," she advised. Jason and Edward sat up.

"What time is it?" Edward asked.

"Edward, you know how to tell time," his mother said, disappearing.

Edward put down his crayon and climbed up onto the table. Both hands of the clock pointed straight up.

"What time is it?" asked Jason.

Edward put his arms straight up over his head.

"Almost time for lunch," said Jason.

Edward sat down again. He and Jason put their chins back on the table. Jason read. Edward drew. Outside, it drizzled. Inside, it was quiet and comfortable.

After a while, Mrs. Fraser came to help the boys make sandwiches. She looked at the footprints on the kitchen table.

"Someone's been walking on the table," she observed, taking the tuna fish out of the fridge.

"Me," said Edward.

"With your shoes on," she noted.

"Usually I take them off," said Edward.

"Usually?" wondered Mrs. Fraser. "Is it usual for you to walk on the table?"

"Only when I need to see what time it is," Edward explained.

Mrs. Fraser looked thoughtful. "You stand on the table to tell the time?" she asked.

"So I can see the clock. The numbers. And the big hand and the little hand," said Edward.

Mrs. Fraser took the bread out of the bread box. She looked even more thoughtful. "Jason," she said, "can you see the words in your book if you pick your chin up?"

"Sure," said Jason.

"How about if you hold your book at arm's length?" asked his mother.

"Yep," said Jason.

"How about in school?" she said. "Can you see the blackboard from the back of the room?"

"I sit in front," Jason said.

"What if you sat in back?" Mrs. Fraser asked.

"Um," Jason said.

"Um, yes?" Mrs. Fraser asked. "Or um, no?"

"Um, sort of."

"Um, sort of?"

"Um, kind of."

"Um, kind of?"

"Mom, I do *not* need glasses!" Jason said.

"I think you might," said Mrs. Fraser. "I'm almost positive Edward does, and I think you might, too."

"Glasses!" Edward said brightly.

"Glasses," Jason said darkly.

"Oh, come on, Jason," Mrs. Fraser said. "Almost everyone has to wear glasses sooner or later."

"Dad doesn't wear them," Jason pointed out. "And neither do you."

"Well, I used to wish I could," said his mother, "back when I was a kid and my sister got everything instead of me. She got braces, and she broke her arm and got all the attention, and she got glasses, too. And I didn't."

Edward made his fingers and thumbs into circles and put them around his eyes. He zoomed around the kitchen, looking at everything. "I see!" he said. "I see!"

Jason looked exasperated. "Edward," he said, "quit that. You don't see. It's not good to wear glasses. It's terrible. Kids don't want to wear glasses."

"They don't?" said Edward, taking down his fingers.

"Of course not," Jason told him. "If you have glasses and you run, they fall off."

"That's not true," Edward said. "Jenny Barnes is the fastest runner in my class, and she has glasses. She keeps them on with a strap when she's playing."

"If you have glasses, people make fun of you," Jason told him. "They call you 'four-eyes.'"

Edward giggled. "'Four-eyes,'" he repeated. "That's pretty funny."

Jason glared at his brother. "It is *not* funny," he said.

A few days later, Mrs. Fraser took Jason and Edward to have their eyes checked. "You boys both are nearsighted," the eye doctor said. "That means you can't see things that are far away. If you were farsighted, you wouldn't be able to see things that were near." She smiled. "Confusing, isn't it?" She handed Mrs. Fraser two prescriptions for eyeglasses. "Jason's vision isn't great," the doctor said. "And Edward is blind as a bat."

Next Mrs. Fraser took Jason and Edward to an eyeglasses store. A woman wearing a white coat was there, ready to help them. She had pink glasses hanging around her neck on a chain. She had a name tag that said "Ms. Applebaum."

"Well," Ms. Applebaum asked, "what can I do for you today?"

Mrs. Fraser handed her the prescriptions. "Both of my boys need glasses," she explained.

"Yeah," said Edward. "I'm blind as a bat."

Ms. Applebaum read the prescriptions. "If your name is Edward," she said, "you certainly are!"

"The first thing you need to do," Ms. Applebaum explained, "is to choose your frames."

Just then the phone rang. "Excuse me," said Ms. Applebaum, "I'll have to get that."

Mrs. Fraser and Jason sat down to wait while she answered the telephone. Edward went over to a display of eyeglass frames and began trying them on. He tried on purple frames and bright red ones. He tried on some tiny gray metal ones. Then he tried on a pair of big black ones, shaped like cat's eyes and decorated with fake diamonds.

"These are the ones I want!" he declared, turning around so his mother and Jason could see.

Jason squinted and stared. Mrs. Fraser laughed. Ms. Applebaum, who had just hung up the phone, frowned. "The children's frames are on the other side of the store," she told Edward. "I think you ought to try on some of those."

"Okay," Edward said. He went over to the other wall where the children's frames were displayed, but he kept the black ones with him.

Ms. Applebaum turned back to Jason. "Now, young man, what about you?"

"Me?" Jason said.

"What kind of frames do you think you'd like?" she coaxed.

"No frames," said Jason. "I'm not getting glasses."

"Oh," said Ms. Applebaum, looking at his prescription, "has there been some mistake?"

"It seems there's about to be," Mrs. Fraser warned Jason.

"I still like these best, Mom," Edward called, waving the cat's-eye frames in his mother's direction. He put them on again. "These are the ones I want."

Jason marched over to Edward and looked down

at him. He looked at the big black glasses covering up three-fourths of his brother's face and at the fake diamonds winking under the bright lights. He took the glasses off Edward's nose. "You can't wear these," he said. "They are ridiculous."

Edward took them back. "I can too wear them," he said. "They are not ridiculous."

Jason grabbed for the frames. Edward hung on. Ms. Applebaum took half a step in their direction. Mrs. Fraser dashed across the store. "Boys!" she cried. "You'll break them!" She took the frames.

"They are not ridiculous," Edward insisted, "and I want them."

"They are ridiculous," Jason argued, "and you can't have them."

Both boys looked at their mother. But she wasn't paying any attention to them. Instead, she was looking in the mirror. She was studying her reflection, and she was smiling. She was wearing the black cat's-eye frames.

Ms. Applebaum took over. "You boys need frames made to fit smaller faces," she told them. "You need frames made especially for young people. I'm sure we can find something just right for both of you."

The boys tried on frames for nearly an hour. Edward liked all of them, so he couldn't decide.

Jason didn't like any of them, so he couldn't decide, either. Finally, Mrs. Fraser and Ms. Applebaum decided.

They chose round brown plastic frames for Edward. They chose black metal frames for Jason.

"Aviator style," Ms. Applebaum pointed out, "like pilots wear."

"Pilots," muttered Jason.

"Pilots!" said Edward.

They all trooped back to the table at the front of the store and sat down. Jason looked at his mother. She was still wearing the cat's-eye frames. "You forgot to take off those ridiculous glasses," he reminded her.

Mrs. Fraser looked into the three-way mirror on one end of the table. She pretended to be surprised. "Oh, so I did!" she said. "Anyway, I don't think they're ridiculous."

"Strange, then," said Jason.

"Or strange," his mother answered, still looking dreamily into the mirror.

"*Odd*, then," Jason said.

"Yes," Mrs. Fraser agreed. "Maybe a little odd."

Jason was satisfied, until he noticed that his mother wasn't taking off the glasses.

"I wonder," Mrs. Fraser said to Ms. Applebaum,

"is it possible to get glasses like this if you don't have a prescription?"

"Of course it is," Ms. Applebaum told her. "I can just order plain plastic lenses for them, without any correction." She thought for a moment. "Or you could just buy the frames and not put any lenses in them. That would be cheaper."

Mrs. Fraser thought about that. "I'd feel silly," she decided, "wearing a pair of empty glasses. Let's make them up with the plain plastic." She handed over the frames.

Jason looked at her as if he thought she'd lost her mind.

Edward looked at her as if he thought she'd made one smart move.

Ms. Applebaum, who seemed tired, looked at her as if she hoped Mrs. Fraser was ready to take her boys and go home.

A few days later, when Jason and Edward and their mother came back, Ms. Applebaum fitted their glasses. Then she gave the boys sports straps to hold the glasses on when they were running around. She gave them each an eyeglass case, too, and said to be sure to call her if there were any problems.

71

Edward put on his glasses. As he walked along the street, he looked around. "Wow!" he said. "Things look bright! Wow!" he said. "Things look clear!"

Mrs. Fraser put on her glasses. As she walked along the street, she looked at herself in the shop windows and turned her head this way and that, to make the fake diamonds sparkle in the sunlight.

Jason put his glasses into his case and put the case in his pocket. As he walked along the street, he looked at his shoes.

Edward wore his glasses all the time. He kept the sports strap on so he didn't have to worry about making sudden moves. Mrs. Fraser wore her glasses all the time, too, even first thing in the morning, when she had on her fuzzy blue bathrobe. Jason wore his glasses when his parents said he had to. He wore them when he was in the classroom, when he was reading or doing homework, and when he was watching TV. "If you want to go around not being able to see at other times," his parents told him, "that's up to you."

So when it was up to him, Jason didn't wear his glasses.

He didn't wear them to his first baseball practice. He didn't even take them along.

When it was time for Jason to leave for practice, he got his baseball mitt and his cap. "I'm going," he told his mother.

She looked up from the book she was reading. "Going where?" she asked.

Jason pointed to his baseball cap. He held up his mitt for her to see. "Oh," she said. " 'Bye. Have fun."

Jason put on the mitt and pounded it with his fist. He pulled at his cap. He squinted down the front hallway at an imaginary batter and an imaginary catcher. "Jason Fraser, world-famous pitcher, waits for the signal, winds up for the pitch," he said in a baseball announcer's voice. Edward came out into the hallway to watch.

"And here comes the pitch!" Jason announced. "It's . . . strike three! The famous Fraser fastball crosses the plate at—at—two hundred and fifty miles an hour. Believe it or not, folks, two hundred and fifty miles an hour, and a perfect strike!"

"Wow!" said Edward. "Do that again!"

"Can't," Jason said, opening the front door, "the world-famous pitcher is never late for practice."

"What are you going to practice?" asked Edward.

"The usual stuff, I guess," said Jason. "Fielding and hitting. And I'll practice my pitching, of course.

And maybe we'll work on stealing bases, if we have time."

"Stealing bases?" asked Edward. "Why would you want to steal the bases? Don't you need them to be there for the games?"

"*Edward*, stop that!" said Jason, slamming the front door behind him as he left.

Edward went down the hall to the family room. "It's Edward Fraser," he said in an excited baseball announcer's voice, "getting ready to read a book! Here he comes, folks. He's picking out a book . . . he's sitting down . . . he's opening it . . . he's—he's reading it, at two hundred and fifty miles an hour! He's reading it so fast, he's already finished it and he's picking out another one . . ."

Edward looked at the wall covered with bookshelves. He chose a large book of his mother's. The book had no pictures and many pages, and every page was filled with reading. Edward sat down on the floor and opened up the book. He stared at it and waited.

Edward saw all his favorite letters and the other letters, too. He saw how they were divided up into words, short ones and long ones. He saw how the words marched across the page from left to right, all facing in the same direction. He knew they were saying something, but he couldn't hear what it was.

Edward closed the book and put it back on the shelf. Then he looked out the window at the dove who'd laid her eggs in the walnut tree in an old nest some other bird had built and wasn't using anymore. The dove sat the way she always did, perfectly still. She was a patient bird who sat there all day and all night, keeping her eggs warm with her body and waiting for them to hatch.

Edward waited with her for a few minutes.

Then he got out some of his own books, the ones he could read because he knew them by heart, and snuggled down with them on the couch.

When Jason got home from his baseball practice, he slammed the front door harder than usual. He threw his mitt against the wall. He threw his cap on the floor. He stomped down to the family room and rolled over the back of the couch onto Edward.

"Hey!" Edward protested, pushing his brother off.

"Hey, what?" said Jason, looking for trouble.

"Watch it," said Edward.

"You watch it," Jason said.

"Shut up," said Edward.

"*You* shut up," yelled Jason.

Mrs. Fraser came into the family room with her

finger on her lips. "Boys!" she warned. "You'll have to go outside if you want to yell, at least until the eggs are hatched." She tiptoed over to the window to see if the dove had been disturbed.

"Do you want to yell?" Edward asked Jason.

"I might," Jason answered.

Edward sighed and closed his book. "Let's go outside, then," he said.

Jason and Edward sat on the front steps. They didn't yell. They didn't even speak. They just sat.

Pretty soon, Mike Lombardi came along the sidewalk on his skateboard. Mike was wearing red high-top sneakers and ragged cutoffs. He was wearing sunglasses.

"Hey, dudes," Mike said, stopping in front of the steps where Jason and Edward sat.

"Hi, Mike," Edward said, pointing to his own face.

"Glasses," Mike observed. "Cool."

"I'm blind as a bat without them," Edward boasted.

"Me too," said Mike, pointing to his sunglasses. "That's why I never appear without shades."

Jason was still gloomy. "Hi, Mike," he finally said.

Mike looked at Jason. "Why so low, bro?" he asked.

"I just found out I won't get to pitch for my baseball team this year," Jason told him. "I can't seem to get the ball over the plate. Alexandra Simpson is pitching."

"They're not going to let you pitch?" asked Edward.

"Not unless I can get the ball under control."

"But what about your two-hundred-and-fifty-mile-an-hour fastball?" Edward wanted to know.

"What about it?"

"Can Alexandra pitch a two-hundred-and-fifty-mile-an-hour fastball?"

"Of course she can't," Jason said. "Nobody can. You should know that."

"What position do you get to play, then?" Edward asked.

"Left field," muttered Jason. "Coach put me out in left field."

"Cheer up, man!" said Mike. "Left field's not so bad. I'm out in left field a lot of the time myself."

"I didn't know you played baseball, Mike," Edward said.

"Shades," Jason mumbled to himself.

Mike smiled at Edward. "What an excellent sense of humor you've got, dude," he said, pushing off. "Later!" he called over his shoulder.

" 'Bye, Mike," called Edward.

Jason stood up. "Shades!" he declared.

Shades would be the solution to his problems, Jason decided. Shades were cool. He wouldn't mind wearing shades one bit. Actually, he might enjoy it. He'd get some just like Mike's.

"A pretty expensive solution" was Mrs. Fraser's first response. But she talked it over with Mr. Fraser, and they decided Jason could have another pair of glasses if he earned part of the cost himself.

"I'll help you," Edward said.

"How?" Jason said.

Edward thought. "You can have my allowance."

"If we put your allowance and mine together, I can save up enough money in about twenty years," Jason told him.

"You could do odd jobs for the neighbors," Mr. Fraser suggested.

Jason and Edward decided to give that a try. Jason made a flyer. It said: "Odd Jobs/Good Workers/Fair Prices." It said: "Call Today." It gave their names and their telephone number.

Mrs. Fraser drove them to the copy shop. She even paid for the copies. Jason and Edward took the flyers around the neighborhood and left them in people's mailboxes. Then they went home and hung around, waiting for the phone to ring.

"It's silly for both of us to wait," Jason said. "Let's take turns."

That was all right with Edward. He got out his Legos and sat right by the telephone while he built a tiny go-cart.

When the phone rang, he answered on the first ring. "I don't know, Mrs. Potter. I'm not sure," Jason heard him say.

Jason rushed to the phone and listened while Mrs. Potter repeated her request. "We'll be there first thing Saturday morning," he told her.

"We're going to do it?" asked Edward.

"Of course we're going to," Jason said. "Why wouldn't we?"

Edward thought, and then he shrugged. "Okay," he said, "but I don't see what's so strange about tying up old papers and carrying them to the curb."

"There isn't anything strange about it," Jason said. "Why should there be?"

"Because we said we wanted to do jobs that were strange," Edward told him. "It says so, right on the flyer you made."

"What are you talking about?" Jason said.

"I'm talking about our flyer. You wrote 'Odd Jobs' on it. And odd is the same as strange. And there's nothing strange about Mrs. Potter's job."

"You know what's odd?" Jason yelled. "You know what's strange? You are, that's what!"

Edward refused to answer.

From then on, the boys accepted every job they were offered. They worked after school and on the weekend. And the only *odd* job they had was taking Rudy Murata's pet white rat for a walk one afternoon when Rudy was sick and couldn't go out. For twenty-five cents, Edward carried the white rat on his shoulder and walked five times around the block.

When they counted their money at the end of the week, Jason said they were getting no place fast. Edward wondered what he meant, but decided not to ask. Instead, he went over to the window to wait with the dove for a bit. But there was no need to wait any longer. The eggs had hatched, and the baby doves, two of them, were tucked underneath their mother's body, just as the eggs had been. The head of one baby dove stuck out in the front, right under the mother's head. The head of the other baby dove stuck out in the back, right under the mother's tail.

"Wow!" said Edward.

Jason looked. "Wow!" he said.

Edward giggled. "It looks like a bird with three heads," he said, "doesn't it, Jason?"

"A bird with three heads," Jason said thoughtfully. "It sure does."

The boys made a big sign on a piece of white poster board. Jason wrote the words: "Come and see this Bird. Adults $1. Kids 50 cents." Underneath Jason's words, Edward drew the picture. He drew what looked like a three-headed bird sitting on a nest. The boys put the poster out in front of their house.

Before long, the doorbell rang. It was Elaine Abrams. "I want to see the bird with three heads," she said, handing Jason fifty cents. Edward took her into the family room. He put his finger to his lips, so Elaine would know she had to be quiet. Then he showed her the dove and her babies. Elaine stared at the birds. "That's not a three-headed bird," she whispered.

"Of course it isn't," Edward said. "There's no such thing." He grinned at Elaine.

Elaine stood quietly and watched the mother bird and her babies for a few minutes. Edward watched with her. While they were standing there, they heard the doorbell ringing and ringing. They heard footsteps on the front porch. They heard voices. Elaine grinned at Edward. "Did you do that on purpose?" she asked.

"Do what on purpose?" asked Edward.

"Did you make the picture look as if the bird has three heads on purpose?"

"Sure," said Edward. "You can see for yourself, the bird does look like she has three heads."

Elaine had to agree.

And so did all the other people who waited in line and paid to see the bird and her babies that afternoon.

The Unexpected

Jason and Edward and their parents were taking a summer vacation. They were not going to Disneyland, like Elaine Abrams and her family, or to the lake, like Jeffrey Sanders and his family. And they were not headed for the ocean, like Tyler Franklin and his family. Jason and Edward and their parents were spending their vacation in a log cabin in the woods.

"Where nobody else is going!" their father declared, showing them the location of the cabin on a big map he'd gotten from the Forest Service. "We'll fish in the streams and hike in the woods, cook over an open fire, and sleep out under the

84

stars if we want to, and not a single soul but us will be there, not for miles around."

"Why?" asked Jason.

"Why what?" answered his father.

"Why will nobody be there but us?"

"Because it's a place that's very hard to get to, for one thing," said Mr. Fraser happily. "And once you get there, no electricity, no indoor plumbing, no TVs or radios or telephones. Just a one-room cabin and a lot of trees, and no other people."

Jason and Edward looked at each other, horrified. "Mom!" they protested.

Mrs. Fraser faked a smile. "Don't worry, boys," she said. "This is going to be a terrific experience for all of us. You hardly ever get a chance these days to live in the wilderness for a week. And besides, it's just this once. Dad promised."

Jason and Edward watched their friend Elaine pack. She took shorts and T-shirts to wear to Disneyland in the daytime. She took her bathing suit to use in the hotel swimming pool. And she took a dress to wear out to dinner. Everything Elaine needed to go to Disneyland for a week fit into a suitcase she could carry by herself.

Jason and Edward visited with their friend Jeffrey while he got his things together to take to the lake.

He took sunscreen and a visor. He took swimming trunks. He took a book called *Power Boating for Kids*. He took a book called *Water Skiing Made Easy*. Everything Jeffrey needed to go to the lake for a week he could carry by himself.

Jason and Edward helped their forgetful friend Tyler get ready for his vacation at the beach. They reminded him to pack his fins and his mask and his snorkel. They wished him good luck in the Sand Castle Building Contest. At the last minute, they stuffed a collecting bag for seashells into his backpack and some surfboard wax into his duffel. Everything Tyler needed to go to the ocean for a week he could carry by himself, if he could just remember it.

At dinner that night, Mr. Fraser reminded them, "Our vacation this year will be an old-fashioned one. We're going to rough it and get back in touch with Mother Nature."

"Elaine is going to Disneyland," Edward said.

"She's staying in a hotel," Jason added.

"Poor Elaine," Mr. Fraser commiserated. "She'll be riding around on mechanical toys and eating all kinds of junk food the whole time she's away. Call that a vacation?"

"Yep," said Edward.

"Well, I don't call it a vacation," his father said.

"Elaine can ride in cars and eat junk food right here at home."

"Jeffrey's going to the lake," Jason said.

"He's going to learn how to water-ski," Edward added, "and his dad promised to let him steer the speedboat, too."

"There they'll be," Mr. Fraser said sympathetically, "out on the lake with a million other boats, breathing in gasoline fumes and getting headaches from the roar of all those engines. Call that a vacation?"

"Yep," said Jason.

"Tyler's going to the ocean," Edward said. "He's going to collect seashells and enter a Sand Castle Building Contest."

"He's going to learn how to snorkel and ride on a surfboard," Jason added.

"That's too bad," said Mr. Fraser, his voice soft with pity. "Tyler will have to take a lot of lessons to learn how to snorkel and surf. He'll hardly have a minute to himself. And think how disappointed he'll feel when the waves break up his sand castle and sweep it out to sea. Call that a vacation?"

"Yep," said Mrs. Fraser, with a sigh.

"*Our* vacation will be different," Mr. Fraser said. "We won't bring junk food with us, so we won't eat any. No place to buy junk food in the woods, you know. Whatever we need to learn we'll have to teach ourselves. Nobody around to give lessons in the wilderness! The air we breathe will be clean and clear. It will be so quiet all day, an insect buzzing will sound like a loud noise. It will be so peaceful at night, an acorn falling to the ground will get our attention. Everything will be *entirely different* from what we're used to here at home. Now, that's what I call a vacation."

What Mr. Fraser said was true. From the very beginning, it was clear this vacation was going to be entirely different. For one thing, it took days of hard work to get ready to go on it. For another, they needed to take many more things with them to live simply in the woods for a week than even Mr. Fraser could possibly carry by himself.

They had to buy things and rent things and borrow things from almost everyone they knew. They needed backpacks and sleeping bags and ground cloths. They needed flashlights with extra batteries and kerosene lanterns with extra wicks. They needed a food cooler to set in the stream. They needed rope. They needed a hatchet. They needed shorts and sleeveless shirts for the blazing-hot days. They needed long underwear for the freezing-cold nights. They needed fishing poles.

They needed strong hiking boots so they wouldn't turn their ankles when they were out on the trails. They needed shrill whistles to blow in case they got lost in the woods. They needed cups to hang on their belts and bandannas to tie around their sweaty foreheads. They needed ponchos in case it rained and sunscreen in case it didn't, and they needed insect repellent in either case. They needed biodegradable soap that wouldn't pollute. And they needed a first-aid kit and a snakebite kit, and some allergy medicines, too. "Just in case," their father said cheerfully.

What they wouldn't need, Mr. Fraser told them, was anything noisy, anything that would interrupt the peace and quiet, anything that would remind them of the hustle and bustle of the world they'd left behind.

"Our cassette players?" Edward wondered.

"No," his father answered.

"My portable radio?" Jason hoped.

"Not a chance," his father said.

"A cordless phone?" Mrs. Fraser wanted to know.

"Certainly not!" Mr. Fraser replied.

Instead of radios playing and telephones ringing and the noise of cars and trucks and sirens, Mr. Fraser explained to them again, they would hear wood crackling in the fire, crickets chirping in the bushes, and deer snuffling at the edge of the forest. They would hear the wind rushing in the trees, the stream splashing over the rocks, and small wild creatures rustling in the tall grass.

"And rattlesnakes rattling," said Jason, looking at the snakebite kit.

"And bears growling," said Edward, looking at the first-aid kit.

"And Jason and Edward arguing," said Mrs. Fraser, looking at the ceiling.

The Frasers bought and rented and borrowed so much stuff, they could barely squeeze into their living room, where it was all stacked.

"No simple matter," Mr. Fraser told them as he surveyed the scene, "going to live in the wilderness for seven days." They had to plan every single thing they would want to eat or use for the entire week. Because, once they got up there, there was no turning back. Whatever they forgot to bring they would have to do without.

They planned and planned. But when they finished, Mr. Fraser reminded them that there was no way in the world to plan for everything that might come up.

"There are bound to be surprises," he told them, smiling broadly, "lots of surprises, both good and bad. But we'll be ready for them. We'll be tough

and resourceful, happy campers—pioneers. Nothing that happens will send *us* packing. We'll stay for the whole week, no matter what. We'll expect the unexpected, take the bad with the good, and be ready for more. What do you say to that?"

Mrs. Fraser saluted. The boys didn't say anything. And Mr. Fraser left to rent a four-wheel-drive Jeep, the only thing he trusted to get them and all their gear safely up the rough roads to their destination.

The drive was long. At the beginning, the overloaded Jeep sped along a wide, straight freeway, along with many other vehicles. Jason and Edward sat stiffly in the back, hemmed in by equipment and provisions.

Mr. Fraser sat tall in the driver's seat, singing as he drove, "She'll be comin' round the mountain when she comes!"

Mrs. Fraser slumped next to him. She had a map open in her lap, but Jason could tell that behind her sunglasses, she was asleep. Mrs. Fraser got sick to her stomach on long car rides, and the medicine she took to prevent car sickness always put her to sleep.

After a while, they turned off the freeway onto a two-lane road, which curved more and more sharply as it began to wind up into the mountains.

On one curve, Mr. Fraser had to edge carefully around a group of bicycle racers, wearing white plastic helmets and shiny, colorful bike clothes with numbers on the backs of their shirts.

"Would you look at that!" Mr. Fraser said admiringly as he watched the riders pump and perspire.

Farther along, Mr. Fraser had to pull almost entirely off the road to let three motorcycle riders storm by. They were dressed in black leather vests and big black boots, and one of them had long hair streaming out behind him. They rode easily, leaning back in a relaxed way as they roared up the narrow road.

"Would you look at that," Mr. Fraser said irritably as he watched them zoom around a curve, and disappear.

Soon the road got steeper and even more curvy.

It was when they were crossing the bridge over the North Fork River that Mrs. Fraser woke up. "Are we almost there?" she begged.

"Well, almost," Mr. Fraser said doubtfully. "Do you need to stop?"

Mrs. Fraser groaned, and Mr. Fraser pulled over as soon as he could.

They parked at a place called Scenic Lookout, where there was a tall waste can chained to a tree, a picnic table with benches attached to it, and a view of treetops spreading down the mountainside into the valley below.

Jason, Edward, and Mr. Fraser ate peanut-butter-and-jelly sandwiches and drank cool lemonade out of a thermos. Mrs. Fraser sucked on grapefruit slices and put her head down on her arms.

After they ate and rested, Jason, Edward, and Mrs. Fraser walked reluctantly back to the Jeep. But Mr. Fraser marched back to it with a spring in his step and a gleam in his eye, singing the next verse of his song, "Oh, she'll have to sleep with Grandma when she comes!"

Hours later, the Frasers pulled into Sierraville, the last little town they would see before they wound up the one-lane fire road that their directions said would take them to the cabin in the woods, where they would have to stay for a whole week, no matter what.

As they came into town, they saw a sign that said: "Population: 352."

"Counting all the dogs and cats," Mrs. Fraser joked weakly.

"I'll bet you're right on the money there," said Mr. Fraser, unable to conceal his joy.

The town of Sierraville had one main street,

which was two blocks long. On that one street were the café, the hardware store, the drugstore, the firehouse, the library, the sheriff's office, the school, which was closed, and the school yard, which was empty. Benches lined the raised wooden sidewalks, and on the benches sat old men wearing overalls and caps. They all turned their heads and squinted at the Jeep in a not very friendly way as it lumbered down the street and parked in front of the hardware store.

Mr. Fraser, Jason, and Edward got out to stretch their legs. Mrs. Fraser stayed in her seat with her head resting on her hand.

A white banner stretched overhead from one side of the street to the other. The banner had huge red letters on it. "WELCOME BIKERS," it said.

"Bikers?" wondered Jason.

"What?" said Edward.

" 'Welcome Bikers,' " Jason read, pointing to the banner so Edward would know what he was talking about.

"I can read it," Edward fibbed.

"What bikers?" Jason asked his father.

"Must be a cross-country bicycle race," Mr. Fraser said. "That would explain all the bike riders with numbers on their shirts. The ones we passed on the road coming up."

"Maybe I should've brought my bike," said Edward.

"With or without the training wheels?" teased Jason.

Edward tried to step on Jason's foot. Jason tried back. Mr. Fraser went into the hardware store to get some extra flashlight batteries. Jason and Edward strolled down the street to the firehouse, where a yellow-haired boy about Jason's age stood straddling a two-wheeler and looking off down the road, as if he expected to see something or someone appear in the distance. Jason and Edward stopped and looked, too.

"What're you watching for?" Jason asked the boy.

"Bikers," he answered.

"The ones in the race?" asked Edward.

"What race?" the boy asked.

"The bicycle race. We passed some of the racers on our way up here."

The boy shrugged. "No bicycle race coming through here," he told them.

"What's that sign for, then?" Jason challenged. "It says right there: 'Welcome Bikers.' "

"I can read," the boy said.

"Well?" said Jason.

"Bikers. *Motorcycle riders*," the boy said impatiently. "The Chopper Chiefs. They hold their annual three-day convention here in Sierraville every summer."

"Chopper Chiefs?" said Jason, his eyes growing wide with interest.

"Indian Chiefs?" Edward wanted to know.

The yellow-haired boy looked at Edward in a way that made him stand a little bit behind his brother.

"A motorcycle riders' convention?" Jason said, trying to get the boy to tell him more. "I never heard of anything like that."

"Well, you have now," the boy said. "There'll probably be about a hundred of them. They'll meet down by the fork in the river and ride in together. Then they'll take over the whole town. And the woods, too. Powwow and race cross-country all day and all night. Party and whoop it up the whole time." The boy grinned. "It's the only thing that happens around here all year long that's worth talking about."

Jason and Edward looked at each other. Motorcycle riders, noisy and wild, racing through the town, roaring through the woods, for three whole days and nights!

"Is there any place they don't go?" Edward asked.

"No place," the boy bragged. "Why, the Chopper Chiefs raise so much dust in the three days and nights they're here, we choke on it just about the whole rest of the summer."

Jason and Edward walked back to the Jeep. "There are bound to be surprises," Jason said, in a voice like his father's.

"Good and bad," Edward said, in a voice like Jason's.

"You have to expect . . ." said Jason, giggling.

"The unexpected!" said Edward, cracking up.

"She'll be wearin' pink pajamas when she comes!" sang Mr. Fraser, shifting the Jeep into low gear so it could labor up the last two steep, crinkum-crankum, rutted miles of unpaved road that led to the cabin.

By the time the Frasers arrived, it was late afternoon. Jason and Edward looked inside the cabin. It was small and dark. It was decorated with spiders' webs. Mr. Fraser looked in, too. "Home sweet home," he said, in a satisfied way.

Then the boys looked out across the sloping meadow. They saw hundreds of dragonflies, the size of tiny birds, skimming over the top of the long, golden grass. "Mother Nature's Mosquito Patrol," their father explained.

While Mrs. Fraser lay down on a sagging old

bunk, Mr. Fraser and the boys unloaded the Jeep.

"Oh, we'll all go out to meet her when she comes!" Mr. Fraser sang under his breath as he carried the heaviest things into the cabin.

"Row, row, row your boat," hummed Edward, taking small loads.

"Shh," said Jason, who thought he heard a hum or a rumble or the whine of an engine off somewhere in the distance.

"That's the spirit, Jason," Mr. Fraser said. "You're already understanding how we are in the woods."

"How are we again?" asked Edward.

"Quieter," Mr. Fraser said. "More attentive. Listening. Listening carefully to the—to the sound of the—quiet."

By the time the Jeep was finally unloaded, Mrs. Fraser felt better. She and Mr. Fraser lit the kerosene lanterns and got busy organizing things inside the cabin. Jason and Edward pulled on their sweatshirts and went outside.

The early evening sky over the mountains was navy blue. A single bright star was out. And the tall, golden grass that covered the meadow seemed to glow.

The boys found an old ropeswing hanging from one of the branches of a large tree. First they took

turns jumping off a stump, holding tight to the thick rope and gliding out over the meadow. Then they rode together, Jason standing up and Edward sitting down, twisting and twirling until they were dizzy.

After that, they sat down with their backs against the trunk of the tree and waited, both of them listening hard—and with mixed feelings now—for the first faint sounds of the unexpected.